ISBN 0-8114-9326-1

4 5 6 7 8 03 02 01 00 99

Produced by Mega-Books of New York, Inc.
Design and Art Direction by Michaelis/Carpelis Design Assoc.

Cover illustration: Ken Spencer

# CHARMERS

by Judy Katschke

interior illustrations by
Joan Holub

STECK-VAUGHN
COMPANY

# Chapter One

Planet Givvon was not a fun place to be for Zakk Givvonson. At least not on this particular day in the 25th century.

"I'm sorry, Zakk," said Nemi Givvonez, his supervisor. "But you're just not ready to be a salesperson."

Zakk couldn't believe it. This was his second summer as a stock boy at Spacey's, Planet Givvon's largest department store. He had always worked his antenna off!

"Why?" asked Zakk.

"Boxer shorts," said Nemi.

"Boxer shorts?" asked Zakk.

"Most people fold the legs of the

shorts first. You fold the shorts. Don't think people don't notice these things, Zakk!" Nemi said.

Zakk was about to reply when Nemi's office door burst open.

"Happy birthday, Zakk!" It was Vora McGivvon, Zakk's girlfriend. Vora worked as a junior sales assistant at the Cosmic Cosmetics counter. Zakk looked at the birthday cake in Vora's outstretched hands.

Nemi jumped up from her chair. "How dare you! What makes you think you can come in here and interrupt my meeting?"

"I thought you'd be finished by now, Nemi," said Vora. "Besides, it's Zakk's seventeenth birthday."

To Vora's horror, Nemi leaned over and blew all the candles out.

"Hey!" shouted Zakk. "That was my wish you just blew out!"

Nemi returned to her desk. "Blowing

out birthday candles is a silly Earth custom!" she said. "How it caught on here on Planet Givvon, I'll never know!"

Vora led Zakk out of Nemi's office. She pointed to the birthday cake. There was one last candle with a flame still bravely flickering. "Make a wish, birthday boy," Vora said.

Zakk closed his eyes and pictured Nemi falling into a crater. He blew out the candle.

"So, did you get the promotion?" asked Vora.

"Do I look like I'm celebrating?" snapped Zakk. He dragged a finger through the frosting.

"Well, don't take it out on me!" said Vora. She stormed back to the cosmetics counter.

Zakk followed her and leaned over the counter. "I'm sorry, Vora. Nemi says I'm not ready to be a salesperson. But I

know that's not the real reason she won't promote me."

"Then what is?" asked Vora. She slid the cake under the counter.

"Nemi and every salesperson in her department split the monthly department bonus," Zakk explained. "So, the fewer salespeople, the more money there is for her."

Vora raised an eyebrow. "Do you think so?"

"I know so!" said Zakk.

Vora smiled and reached into her pocket.

"This will cheer you up," Said Vora as she pulled out a shimmering crystal.

"Is this a Rockhounds find?" asked Zakk. Vora was a rock collector and president of the Rockhounds Club at their school.

Vora nodded. "It's a crystal I got on our last collecting trip."

Zakk stared down at the crystal.

"Hey!" he cried. "It's changing colors!"

"It changes into 1,000 different colors," boasted Vora. "But it does a lot more than just that." Vora slipped the stone into Zakk's hand.

Suddenly, Zakk began to feel his spirits lift. He was in a great mood!

"Cool!" Zakk whistled. Losing the promotion didn't seem so tragic.

Vora beamed. "What's even cooler is that I found a way to grow more crystals just like it in my backyard. I just chip off a piece and spray it with my secret formula . . ."

"Miss!" shouted a customer.

"May I help you?" asked Vora, turning to the customer.

"This makeup powder you sold me yesterday is wrong!" The Givvonite slammed a compact on the counter.

Vora read the label. "You weren't happy with Galaxy Green No. 5?"

"It was more like Guacamole Green

No. 5!" shouted the customer. "I want the manager!"

"Please!" said Vora. "I'm sure I can help you."

"Manager! Manager!"

"Oh, great," mumbled Vora.

"Hey, no problem," Zakk smiled. He quickly slipped the crystal into the angry customer's hand. "Hold this for me, will you?"

"I beg your pardon?" snapped the customer. Zakk and Vora watched as the customer's face brightened. In no time a smile had replaced her scowl.

"How lovely," she giggled.

Nemi came hurrying up to the counter.

"Someone call for the manager?" she asked, glaring at Vora.

"I did," smiled the customer.

"Is there a problem?" Nemi asked.

"Oh, no!" the customer answered. "I just wanted to let you know what a wonderful job this girl is doing!"

Vora smiled. "Why, thank you!"

"In fact," the customer said, "I want to buy five compacts of Guacamole Green No. 5."

Nemi squinted. "Guacamole?"

While Vora beamed the customer's money through the cash-o-meter, Nemi turned to Zakk.

"Don't you have boxes to unpack?"

Zakk picked the crystal up from the counter and tossed it at Nemi.

"Catch!" he said.

"What are you . . .?"

Nemi caught the crystal. Just as she was about to toss it back to Zakk, she froze. Zakk watched in amazement as

the corners of Nemi's mouth drew up in a smile.

"Man!" thought Zakk. "If that crystal can work on Nemi, it can work on anybody!"

"Wow!" Nemi thought. "Is this what it's like to be . . . happy?"

She whirled around to Zakk. "Zakk!" Nemi said. "It's your birthday. Why don't you go home early."

Zakk stared at his supervisor.

"With pay!" Nemi added.

"Thanks, Nemi!" said Zakk. "But before I leave, may I have my birthday present back?"

"Your birthday present?" asked Nemi.

"The crystal," said Zakk. "Vora grew it in her backyard."

"That Vora," Nemi smiled. She handed the crystal back to Zakk.

"See you tomorrow!" Zakk called over his shoulder. He reached behind the counter and got his cake.

Nemi stared as Zakk headed out the door. She shook her head in confusion. "What did I just do?" she thought.

# Chapter
# Two

Vaydal Drumm had always dreamed of being a space cadet. But that dream included rocketing to distant planets, not working in Product Control at Station Earth Port!

Still, Vaydal was determined to do well. If anyone could regulate products going into Planet Earth, he could.

That morning Vaydal was sitting face to face with yet another alien promoting a product. The alien was about two and a half feet tall, with a large bumpy head and three tiny eyes.

"Please describe your product in five minutes," Vaydal instructed.

"It's a set of goggles that can detect vehicles in space!" said the alien. "They allow you to see incoming space vehicles from a great distance." The alien whipped the goggles out of his sack.

Vaydal looked at the goggles closely. "Sir," he asked. "What planet are you from?"

"Mars!" boasted the Martian.

"May I ask a question?" asked Vaydal. "How many eyes do I have?"

"How many eyes?" repeated the Martian.

Vaydal smiled and nodded.

The Martian stared at Vaydal. "You have two eyes."

"And how many eyes do these goggles have?" cried Vaydal.

"Three," the Martian mumbled.

"Earthlings have two eyes," said Vaydal. "Count them. Two!"

"But, don't you want to hear about

the goggles' features?" the Martian pleaded.

"Next!" Vaydal called.

The Martian grabbed the goggles and his sack and dashed out the door.

Vaydal turned to his co-workers, Tresta and Bowan.

"Why don't aliens research Earth before trying to do business here?"

"You're too tough!" laughed Bowan from behind his desk. "You'd even reject a Happy Face!"

A messenger walked into the chamber carrying a package.

"Satellite Express!" he said. "Delivery from Planet Givvon."

Vaydal signed for the package. "Who wants it?"

"I'm only taking it if it's something to eat," said Tresta.

"What else is new?" grinned Bowan.

Vaydal placed the box on a silver tray and pulled a switch. The box disappeared to reveal a smaller metal box inside.

"Another box," Vaydal sighed.

Bowan grabbed the box off the pedestal. "Will Vaydal go for the box?" he joked. "Or for the curtain?"

Tresta swept her hand across an imaginary curtain.

Suddenly the metal box snapped open

in Bowan's hands. Vaydal reached in and pulled out a note.

"'You have just become the proud owner of an original Charmer Ring,'" he read. "'Put it on. The colors aren't the only things that change!'"

Tresta pulled out a ring from the box and slipped it on her finger. "I wonder what that means?"

"There's only one way to find out,"

said Bowan, taking a ring.

"Before we start making fashion statements," said Vaydal, "let's check these rings more carefully."

"What's to check?" cried Bowan, his face beaming. "I feel great, and that's all that really matters!"

Bowan jumped up on his desk and

began singing. "I feeeel good! . . ."

"Bowan!" cried Vaydal.

"Wow!" exclaimed Tresta. "This thing works better than a pint of Jupiter Almond Fudge Soy Cream!"

Bowan grabbed a bunch of rings and tossed them around the office.

"Compliments of Planet Givvon, guys!" he called out.

"Will you please calm down?" Vaydal snapped. "There are aliens waiting outside!"

"So what?" laughed Bowan.

"Come on, Vaydal!" smiled Tresta. "Try one on."

"Yeah, Vaydal," said Bowan, tossing him a ring. "Go for it!"

Vaydal caught the ring.

"It is beautiful," he said, slowly slipping it on his pinky.

"Well?" asked Tresta.

Vaydal sighed. A marvelous feeling surged through his body.

"Hmmmmm," said Vaydal. "So are you going to approve it?" asked Bowan.

"Not yet," said Vaydal. "It needs to be studied and tested."

"If you won't approve it, pal," said Bowan, "I will."

Vaydal stared at his friend. They often had disagreements. But they never overruled each other.

"Fine," said Vaydal.

Bowan smiled and turned to the other cadets.

"Is everybody happy?" he called.

Vaydal leaned back in his chair. He gazed at the dazzling jewel.

"Nice . . . very nice," thought Vaydal.

Then he yanked the ring off his finger and dropped it in his desk drawer. "But I've got work to do."

Vaydal turned to the door and shouted. "Next!"

# Chapter Three

"I told you!" cried Zakk. "We don't carry Stardust-busters!"

"Well!" said the frustrated customer as he huffed away.

Zakk leaned on the boxes of Mercury motor-mops he was unpacking.

"What's gotten into me?" he wondered. He had never yelled at a customer before.

"Hi, Zakk." It was Vora.

"Just the person I want to see," said Zakk. He reached into his pocket and pulled out the crystal.

"Is there a guarantee on this thing?" he asked.

"Oh, no!" said Vora. "Don't tell me you're having a reverse reaction, too!"

"What do you mean?" asked Zakk.

"The same thing happened to my poor little Colette," said Vora.

"Your Givvonese poodle?"

Vora nodded. "Two days ago I attached a crystal to her collar. At first she was friskier than ever. But now she's out of control!"

"Colette?" asked Zakk. "She's a cotton ball with eyes."

"Now she's a snarling brute," groaned Vora.

"Why don't you just pluck the crystal off?" asked Zakk.

"Are you crazy?" cried Vora. "I'd rather pluck a grey hair from the head of Nemi Givvonez!"

Zakk whistled. "That bad, huh?"

"Hello, Zakk. Hello, Vora." Nemi was walking towards them.

"Speak of the devil," Vora mumbled.

"Zakk, will you meet me in the Energy Food Court during your break?"

Zakk gulped, remembering the Stardust-buster scene. "Sure, Nemi."

"I'd like you to join us, too, Vora," Nemi said with a smile.

The pair watched Nemi leave. "I'm confused," said Vora.

"I'm history," sighed Zakk.

\*\*\*

"About the Stardust-busters, Nemi," Zakk began as he and Vora sat down at Nemi's table.

"I just quit Spacey's!" Nemi interrupted Zakk.

"You what?" gasped Vora.

"I just quit Spacey's," laughed Nemi. "Congratulate me."

"But Nemi," said Zakk. "You're a big cheese here!"

"And I'm about to get bigger!"

"What are you going to do?" asked Vora. She looked confused.

"You are now looking at the President of Charmers, Incorporated," said Nemi.

"Never heard of it," said Zakk.

"Of course not," said Nemi. "I just started it!" Nemi pulled a ring from her bag and placed it on the table. "Meet the Charmer Ring!" she exclaimed.

Vora stared at the crystal set in the ring. "That's just like the crystal I gave Zakk for his birthday!"

"But you never thought of giving it to him like this!" said Nemi.

Zakk reached out, took the Charmer

Ring, and slipped it on his finger.

"I plan to sell thousands like it," said Nemi. "Soon every Givvonite will want one. And I'll be there to sell them."

Vora thought of Colette and shuddered. "Nemi . . ." she began.

"These rings are going to sweep Planet Givvon and the entire universe!" whispered Nemi.

"The universe?" asked Zakk.

"Yes!" said Nemi. "I sent Planet Earth some samples a few days ago. And they're already interested!"

Nemi pulled a sheet of paper from her bag. "See? It's the approval from Station Earth Port, signed by Space Cadet Bowan Finch."

Zakk squinted at Nemi. "So why are you telling us?" he asked.

"For one thing, I understand Vora here is quite the little gardener," said Nemi.

"Oh, I get it," sneered Vora. "You want

me to grow the crystals."

"You're not interested?" asked Nemi.

"That's not the point," Vora replied. "How do you know these crystals are actually safe?"

Nemi smiled. "I intend to do a thorough safety check before shipping more rings to Planet Earth."

"Well, I'll have to think about it," Vora said slowly.

"Of course, I can always grow the

crystals myself," said Nemi.

"Not if you don't have my formula," scoffed Vora.

"Who says I don't?" replid Nemi.

"Where did you get these crystals, anyway?" Zakk chimed in.

"Nemi Givvonez!" cried Vora. "You spied on me . . . and probably ripped off some of my crystals, too!"

"You have a lovely garden, Vora," Nemi smiled. "But if I were you, I'd put that miserable little fuzz-ball on a chain."

Zakk snickered as Nemi revealed her bandaged ankle.

"As for you, Zakk," Nemi continued, "how would you like to quit Spacey's and work for a bigger and better company?"

"Oh, sure," groaned Zakk. "I'm just dying to unpack bigger and better boxes."

"As Assistant Director of Marketing?" Nemi added. "You'll work directly with me in spreading the word about these Charmer Rings."

"Assistant Director of Marketing?" Zakk repeated. "I'm in! That is, until school starts."

"Welcome aboard!" Nemi smiled.

Vora stared at Zakk. She and Zakk had been a team for most of their lives. They'd been friends since they were five years old. They went to the same schools. They had even worked at the same part-time jobs.

"If I decide to join this company," said Vora slowly, "what exactly would I be doing? What would my job be?"

"Oh, there'll be lots of stones to cultivate once the orders start blasting in," said Nemi.

"Sounds like grunt work to me," muttered Vora.

"Take it or leave it," Nemi sighed.

Vora looked at Zakk.

"Okay, I'm in," said Vora.

Nemi smiled. She stood up from the table and collected her things.

"Trust me," she said. "These new Charmer rings will be even bigger than . . . the Planet Earth Happy Face!"

Nemi handed Zakk and Vora each a sheet of paper. "Here are your contracts," she said. "Read them. Sign them . . . and have a nice day."

# Chapter Four

By the following week, Charmers, Incorporated was operating out of a small glass domed building, not far from Spacey's.

Zakk and Vora watched as a satellite camera crew set up inside Nemi's office.

"Our first Charmer infommercial!" Nemi exclaimed.

"But Planet Givvon already knows about the Charmers," said Zakk.

"These infommercials aren't just going to our Planet Givvon, silly," said Nemi. "We're beaming them to Planet Earth. We've got to spread the word."

Nemi pointed to a glamorous

Earthling standing nearby. "And look who I invited to Givvon to promote the rings—Elizabeth Tyler! She's also bringing out a new perfume called Four-Alarmer Charmer."

Vora picked up a red feathered scarf that was draped over Nemi's chair. "What is this thing?" she asked.

"Earthlings call it a boa," Nemi

smiled. "Liz gave it to me to wear on the air! You like?"

Vora stared at the scarf and quickly changed the subject. "How are the safety tests coming along, Nemi?"

"Oh, fine," Nemi mumbled. "Which reminds me, Vora. I plan to deliver fifty thousand rings to Earth by next week."

"Yeah, so?" asked Vora.

"So go on, girl. Start pushing up those stones." Nemi chuckled.

"You want me to grow fifty thousand crystals?" cried Vora.

"I plan to launch three autopilot delivery spaceships to Earth," Nemi explained. "Each spaceship can carry about 17,000 Charmer Rings."

"How do you expect me to grow fifty thousand crystals all by myself?" asked Vora. She was steaming.

"You figure it out."

Vora glared at Nemi. "Listen, unless I get more help, I'll . . ."

"You'll what?" asked Nemi. "Go back to Spacey's department store?"

Vora didn't answer.

Nemi laughed wickedly. "Do I have to remind you that you and Zakk have contracts?"

Zakk and Vora stared at each other.

"Until school begins you two are committed to Charmers, Incorporated."

"Five minutes, Ms. Givvonez!" called the infommercial director.

Nemi stood up. She swung the feather boa around her neck.

"Well, kids?" she asked. "What do you think?"

"Drop dead," muttered Vora.

"What?" cried Nemi.

"Drop-dead gorgeous," Zakk said. "We think you look drop-dead gorgeous."

"I suppose I do!"

"And those feathers really suit you, Nemi," Vora said. "Buzzard, aren't they?"

It had been ten days since the cadets of Station Earth Port had first slipped on their Charmer rings—all except Vaydal Drumm.

"Tell me about your product in five minutes or less," Vaydal told a business alien from Planet Neptune.

"It's a pair of shoes that allow Earthlings to defy gravity!" the Neptunian beamed.

"Why would we want to defy gravity?" asked Vaydal.

"Haven't you ever had the urge to walk on the ceiling?" aked the alien.

"Not unless I wanted to dance with a horsefly!" said Vaydal. "Besides, these weren't designed for Earthling feet. We would fall right out of these shoes and onto our heads."

The Neptunian sighed. "You Earthlings don't have any desire to see the world from a new perspective."

"Sorry," said Vaydal.

The Neptunian nodded and left.

Vaydal slumped in his chair. "If I don't get to rocket around soon, I won't need special shoes to climb the walls." Vaydal thought. He opened his desk drawer and spotted the Charmer Ring. That would lift his spirits.

"A whole new perspective, huh?" Vaydal toyed with the ring. "Maybe that's what I need."

"Hey, Vaydal!" Bowan called out. "Get over here, pal!"

Vaydal dropped the Charmer back in his drawer and walked over to Bowan's desk. Bowan was sitting with an alien from Planet Glux.

"Check it out," Bowan smiled. "This guy invented a spray that will keep Earth trees from shedding their leaves."

"You don't say!" Vaydal said.

"Summer all year long," the alien said. He winked. "Give it a shot!"

"Nice," Vaydal said. "But is it environmentally safe?"

"Who cares?" said Bowan. "It's a great product isn't it?"

"How can you say that?" Vaydal protested to his friend.

Bowan shot up from his chair and shouted. "Get off my case, man!" Then the angry cadet picked up his chair and threw it across the room.

The frightened Gluxian shot under the desk.

"Bowan!" shouted Vaydal.

"What?" Bowan shrugged. He sat down as though nothing had happened. "Where's my guy from Glux?"

Vaydal turned to the other cadets. They were all laughing.

"These rings are making people crazy," Vaydal said to himself.

He ran back to his desk and dug out the order slip from the Charmer samples.

"Sent by Ms. Nemi Givvonez," he read. Vaydal smiled.

"Well, Ms. Givvonez," said Vaydal. "You are about to hear from one uncharmed customer!"

# Chapter Five

"Welcome to Charmer Day!" Nemi shouted into the microphone.

She stood on a raised platform in front of three Charmer autopilot delivery spaceships bound for Earth. They were each stocked with 17,000 Charmer Rings.

"In a few minutes we'll be blasting our Charmer Rings to Planet Earth, so let the Charmer festivities begin!" Nemi cried out.

A chorus of young Givvonites broke into song. The happy crowd feasted on thousand-color Charmercones.

Zakk and Vora watched from the

sides of the platform. They weren't cheering.

"I just know she didn't test those rings, Zakk," Vora said. "I know it!"

"You're right. Weird things are happening," whispered Zakk. "A Givvon

spaceball team attacked their opponents from Saturn after losing a game!"

"Really?" asked Vora.

"Yeah. And it just happened to be Charmer Day at the stadium!"

"Well, get this," Vora said. "A sweet Givvonite grandmother went ballistic at a bingo game. Her card markers just happened to be her 'lucky' Charmer crystals!"

"I can't believe we're a part of this," moaned Zakk.

Vora glared at Zakk. "We? I wouldn't have joined this stupid company if it weren't for you!"

Just as Zakk was about to protest, he and Vora heard Nemi's wrist communicator begin to beep.

"Who could be calling me now?" Nemi groaned. She waved at the chorus to stop singing and flicked on her communicator. "Charmers, Incorporated!" she sighed.

"Nemi Givvonez?"

"Speaking," Nemi said.

"This is Cadet Vaydal Drumm from Station Earth Port."

"Earth?" squealed Nemi. She turned to the crowd. "Listen, everybody! It's Earth! It's our most valued customer!"

The crowd cheered. Nemi held the microphone to the communicator.

"Are you about to launch those rings

to Earth?" asked Vaydal.

Nemi winked at the crowd. "Today's the day, Cadet Drumm!"

"Well, you'd better hold off." Nemi turned pale.

The crowd leaned forward to hear more. Nemi pushed the microphone aside and turned her back toward them.

"What did you say?" she whispered.

"The rings have had a strange effect

on my crew," Vaydal explained. "Really strange!"

"Listen, a deal is a deal!" Nemi hissed. "Those Charmers are blasting off for Earth today! Let's go!"

Nemi ripped the communicator off her wrist and faced the crowd.

"Guess what?" she laughed. "Planet Earth said we'd better blast off right away!"

The crowd roared. Zakk and Vora ran over to Nemi.

"Nemi, please hold back on the shipments," Vora begged.

"As far as I'm concerned, honey, your job is done," Nemi said coldly.

Vora angrily watched Nemi catch a bouquet of Givvon lilies.

"That's what you think," mumbled Vora as she walked away.

"Now, fellow Givvonites!" Nemi shouted into the microphone. "Shall we launch the spacecrafts?"

Followed by Zakk and a squad of Givvonite officials, Nemi strutted over to the automatic spaceships.

"Wait!" she cried. "I have a super idea! I want to ride into Earth in one of these vehicles!"

"Nemi, these delivery spaceships don't need pilots," said Zakk.

"I insist!" Nemi said. "If these rings are going to explode upon the scene, I want to be a part of it."

Nemi quickly lowered herself into Spacecraft 3.

Vora and Zakk watched the spaceships blast off.

"We've got to do something!" Vora demanded.

"Got any charming ideas?" Zakk asked glumly.

# Chapter Six

Vaydal was worried. Since he had no luck stopping the shipments, the rings were very likely on their way.

"Tresta," he said. "How long does it take to travel from Planet Givvon to Earth?"

"About a day," Tresta said. "Why?"

"No reason," Vaydal answered quickly. "Thanks, Tresta."

"Don't mention it," Tresta smiled as she bit into a Vanilla Venus Nature bar.

Vaydal watched Tresta very closely. There had been no other outbursts since Bowan's tantrum, but Vaydal wasn't taking any chances.

He slipped into the contact chamber and sat down behind the control panel. He entered the code for his supervisor, Captain Ling. In a few seconds the captain appeared on a large screen.

"What is it, Drumm?" he asked.

"Sir, I'm concerned about the Charmer Rings," said Vaydal.

The captain raised his pinky to the screen and smiled. "You mean this?"

"Oh, great," thought Vaydal.

"My wife got it at a Liz Tyler benefit," he said. "Unfortunately she had to buy that Four-Alarmer Charmer perfume too. That stuff stinks!"

"Sir, I believe the Charmer Rings are dangerous," said Vaydal.

"Dangerous?" asked the captain.

"Yes, sir," said Vaydal. "I believe that in due time, the rings produce a reverse reaction."

The captain raised an eyebrow. "In other words, this groovy feeling may not last?"

"Exactly, sir!" said Vaydal.

The captain scratched his head. "I see. Very interesting, Drumm."

"Three automatic spaceships are already on their way with over 50,000 Charmer Rings," Vaydal explained. "We must stop them!"

"Stop them?" cried Captain Ling. "Drumm, are you mad?"

"Sir?"

"Do you know how many people on this planet saw the Liz Tyler infommercial? Do you know how many people are already demanding their Charmer Rings? Presidents! World leaders! Rock stars!"

"But, sir!" cried Vaydal. "The results may be devastating!"

The captain threw back his head and laughed. "Lighten up, Drumm! And let's put a ring on every finger."

Vaydal watched in despair as the captain faded from the screen.

"There's only one thing to do," he thought. "I've got to stop those shipments from reaching Earth!"

When Vaydal opened the door, the entire cadet crew was staring at him.

"Who were you talking to?" asked Bowan. He glared at the cadet.

Vaydal answered slowly. "I had to speak to Captain Ling."

"About what?" asked Tresta.

"Look," said Vaydal. "These Charmer Rings are dangerous."

"This Charmer is the best thing that's ever happened to me!" shouted Bowan.

"You can disagree with me all you

want!" shouted Vaydal. "But I'm going to stop those rings!"

"If you remember, pal," said Bowan, "I already approved them."

"Come on, Vaydal," laughed Tresta. "Put on a ring and let's party!"

Vaydal wearily shook his head. "Let's party!" Tresta repeated.

"No, Tresta," Vaydal said.

Tresta glared at him. "I *said*, let's party!"

Tresta turned to the nearest desk. With a sweep of her hand she knocked the contents onto the floor. "Let's party!" she screamed. "Let's party! Let's party! Let's party!!"

Tresta began to shake uncontrollably. Vaydal grabbed her and held her until she calmed down.

"Are you okay?" Vaydal asked.

Tresta looked at Vaydal with surprise. "Sure," she laughed. "Why do you ask?"

"Here we go again," Vaydal mumbled. He caught a glimpse of the crystal shimmering on Tresta's hand.

"There is no way those Charmers are entering this planet," he thought to himself. "Not if I can help it!"

# Chapter Seven

"On our show today are three Givvonites whose lives have been changed by Charmer Rings," said Opal Givvonfrey. Opal was the most popular satellite talk show host on Planet Givvon.

"I'm excited to add that our show today will be seen on Planets Earth and Mars!" Opal led the audience in loud applause.

"Our guests today are Zakk Givvonson, Vora McGivvon, and Ida Givvonski," said Opal. "All proud owners of Charmer Rings."

"Fake Charmer Rings," Vora leaned

over and whispered to Zakk.

Opal smiled at Ida. "Ida, let's start with you. How has your life been changed by your Charmer Ring?"

"Oh, Opal!" Ida said. "Before the Charmer Ring, I was a mess!"

"In what way?" asked Opal.

"I was sluggish, my vision was blurred, and my antenna drooped!"

"Sounds like our cameraman, Sy," Opal joked.

"But as soon as my husband gave me my Charmer Ring," continued Ida, "it was like crawling out of a tar pit!"

Opal dabbed her eyes with a handkerchief. "It's stories like yours that make my job so worthwhile."

The talk show host then turned to Zakk and Vora. "Zakk and Vora, you two are best friends, am I right?"

"We go back awhile," said Vora.

"I should say you do!" Opal smiled. "I understand that the Charmer Rings led you to discover that you were really twins separated at birth! . . ."

"No, Opal," said Zakk.

"No?" asked Opal.

"That's just the story we used to get on your show," said Vora.

Opal gulped. "What?"

"What we really want to tell your viewers is that the Charmer Rings are

bad news!" said Zakk.

The audience started to boo.

"What do you mean, 'bad news'?" cried Opal.

"They eventually make Givvonites do crazy things," Zakk continued.

"And they're probably doing the same thing to the poor cadets on Station Earth Port," added Vora.

"Station Earth Port?" asked Opal.

"Yes," said Vora. "They received samples of the Charmer Rings a little over two weeks ago."

Zakk jumped up from his seat. "There are over 50,000 Charmer Rings on their way to Earth now! We want to warn the people of Planet Earth to stay away from those rings!"

Opal smiled at the camera. Then she turned to Zakk and Vora. "This show is supposed to be uplifting."

"I don't know what they're talking about, Opal," said Ida sweetly. "My

Charmer Ring has changed my life!"

Ida suddenly leapt from her chair. She pointed a finger at Vora and Zakk. "Do you hear me, you little punks?" she yelled. "Changed my life!"

The audience gasped as Ida ran up to the camera. She pressed her face against the lens and began to shout, "And another thing! I want more closeups! I didn't get my hair tinted for

nothing! And after the show, I want an assortment of fresh . . ."

Vora gently pulled Ida away and looked into the camera. "See what we mean, folks?"

*** 

Back at Station Earth Port, Vaydal had decided the only way to stop the vehicles from reaching Earth would be to disintegrate them into a million little pieces.

"I've got to get to the control panel where the disintegration switch is," thought Vaydal.

Vaydal noticed that Bowan had made himself comfortable behind the control panel. He was resting his feet dangerously on the rows of switches.

"Bowan, I need to take over for a few minutes," Vaydal said.

"Vaydal, my man!" Bowan laughed. "Do you think I was born yesterday? Do you think I don't know what you're planning to do?"

"What am I planning to do?" Vaydal challenged.

"You want to destroy the incoming spacecrafts," said Bowan. "The ones with the Charmer Rings!"

The other cadets were looking on.

"I'm afraid you're out of luck, buddy," said Bowan. He reached under his chair and pulled out a long metal rod. Bowan began smashing it against the control panel.

"Hey! Knock it off, Bowan!" shouted Vaydal.

Tresta picked up a shattered piece of red plastic. It was the disintegration switch!

"I think he already has, Vaydal," Tresta giggled.

The other cadets laughed along with Tresta. Vaydal returned to his desk and buried his face in his hands.

"Hi," came a voice. "I'm back."

Vaydal looked up to see the Martian who had come by weeks ago. He was holding the goggles in his hands.

"You might want to reconsider my product," the Martian said.

"Not now!" groaned Vaydal.

"Oh, but you must!" insisted the Martian.

Vaydal grabbed the goggles. "It still has three eyes!"

"Forget the eyes!" cried the Martian. "Consider what it can do!"

"You have five minutes to explain what it can do!" Vaydal snapped.

"As I offered to inform you last time," began the Martian, "these goggles help Earthlings spot any spacecraft they wish to manipulate—spacecrafts a million miles away!"

Vaydal straightened up in his chair. "Did you say manipulate? As in control?"

"Affirmative."

Vaydal peered at the Martian. "And once these spacecrafts are spotted, how

does one manipulate them?"

"I thought you'd never ask." The Martian pulled a box from his sack. It was covered with switches and knobs.

He leaned toward Vaydal and whispered. "This is exactly what you need to keep those Charmers from reaching your planet!"

Vaydal pulled the Martian closer. "How'd you know about the Charmers?"

The Martian smiled. "I saw it on Opal."

# Chapter Eight

Vaydal secretly ushered the Martian into an isolated chamber. The small room was equipped with a large window and dozens of radar controls.

"How do the goggles feel?" asked the Martian.

"Foolish," Vaydal mumbled. "And I don't see any space vehicles."

"As soon as they're within a million-mile radius, you will."

Within minutes, Vaydal spotted a spacecraft.

"I see something!" he whispered. "It's a Givvonite autopilot spacecraft! And it's headed our way!"

The Martian shoved the box into Vaydal's hand.

"What do I do?" asked Vaydal.

"Activate the crimson conversion apparatus!" cried the Martian.

"The what?" Vaydal cried.

"Push the red button!"

Vaydal followed the Martian's instructions. Through the goggles he could see that he had stopped the vehicle in its course.

"Now what?" asked Vaydal.

"Pull down the green switch next to your right hand!" said the Martian.

Vaydal quickly pulled the switch and whistled. The spacecraft spun around before shooting out of sight.

"Where did I send it?" asked Vaydal.

The Martian shrugged. "The universe is a very big place."

A knock came on the door.

"Hey, Vaydal!" boomed Bowan's voice. "What are you up to now?"

Vaydal turned to the Martian. "There are two more spacecrafts to go. We've got to work fast!"

The Martian nodded. "Do you see the second one?"

Vaydal adjusted the goggles. "Yeah, there it is!"

"Take it away!" the Martian smiled.

Vaydal did exactly what he had done before. Soon the second vehicle was hurled through space.

"Two down," said Vaydal. "One to go!"

\*\*\*

Nemi sat inside Spacecraft 3, surrounded by boxes of Charmer Rings. She was practicing her arrival speech.

"So I said to myself, 'If I can assure peace and harmony throughout the universe . . .'"

All of a sudden she felt a jolt.

"What was that?" Nemi gasped.

She screamed as Spacecraft 3 broke into a violent spin. Boxes of Charmer Rings tumbled onto the floor.

Nemi tried to calm herself. "It's just some meteoroids," she chuckled.

Then with brutal speed, the vehicle blasted off in another direction, taking

Nemi with it.

"Aaaaaaaaaahhhhhhhhhhhhhh!!"

***

Vaydal sighed and removed the goggles. "That should do it!"

As Vaydal shook the Martian's hand, the door swung open.

Bowan and the other wild-eyed cadets began filing into the chamber.

"I guess my approval doesn't mean much to you, huh, Drumm?"

Vaydal stood and faced Bowan.

"Let's discuss this calmly."

"What's to discuss?" asked Bowan, reaching out for the box. He lifted it above his head and sent it crashing to the floor.

"Unfavorable!" cried the Martian.

Vaydal stood frozen as the cadets stormed forward.

"Very disagreeable predicament," whispered the Martian.

"What?" hissed Vaydal.

"Bad vibes!" the Martian gulped.

Vaydal ducked just in time to avoid a punch. He turned to the Martian.

"Don't you carry a ray gun?"

"You watch too many cartoons!" cried the Martian, giving Bowan a swift karate kick.

Bowan clutched his knee in pain. "Get

them!" he shouted.

The cadets moved in on Vaydal and the Martian.

Vaydal realized the only way out would be through the window. He and the Martian had a better chance of surviving the broken glass than they did the anger of the cadets.

He scooped up the Martian and jumped onto the metal window sill.

"When I count to three, we dive!" whispered Vaydal.

"Through the glass?" cried the Martian.

"One . . . two . . ."

"Freeze!" came a stern voice.

The cadets turned to see the Space Guard standing at the door.

"Yes!" cheered Vaydal.

The guards quickly sprayed the crazed cadets. They used a nontoxic temporary paralyzing chemical. In a few seconds all the cadets stood as frozen as statues.

"Get the rings!" ordered the commanding guard.

Vaydal sighed with relief as he watched the menacing rings finally being removed.

"Now, how do you suppose they knew?" Vaydal asked the Martian.

A guard overheard Vaydal and winked. "We saw it on Opal!"

\*\*\*

"Zakk, Vora, on behalf of my planet, I hope you are enjoying your trip to Earth," said the newly promoted Lieutenant Vaydal Drumm. "It's our way of saying thanks."

"Thank you, Lieutenant Drumm." Vora smiled. "We're having a blast!"

"Yeah! We especially liked your Grand Canyon," said Zakk. "That's the biggest crater we've ever seen!"

"Funny," said Vaydal. "That's what the Martian said, too."

"Zakk and I wish we could stay longer, but we have to start school next week," said Vora.

"Well, there's still time for us to beam over to the Statue of Liberty," Vaydal suggested. He rubbed his hands." As soon as we get there, we'll grab some

good ol' New York style hot dogs and
onion rings!"

"Rings?" Zakk gulped.

"Did you say rings?" Vora stammered.

"On the other hand," Vaydal smiled,
"why don't we skip the onion rings? Hot
dogs for everyone!"